The Waltz

A Dramatic Poem

By

Mark A. F. Bond

ISBN: 9798871971765

First Published in the United States of America by China Doll Publishing
Library of Congress Cataloguing-in-Publication Data, The Waltz
No paragraph, section or chapter of this publication may be reproduced, copied or transmitted save with written permission and in accordance with the provisions of the Copyright protections of the United States.

©1994 Editorial Selection, China Doll Publishing and Mark A. F. Bond.

Table of Contents

The Waltz

The Waltz: Prologue	5
Gilgamesh	6
The Flight	7
Mycenaean Queen	8
Necromancer	9
The Sacrifice	11
The Awakening	12
Atropine	13
God's Ire	14
Late Night Dream	16
Temptation	17
Evil's Journey	18
Valkyrie	20
Odalisque	21
Questions	23
The Dream	25
Forgive	27
Back To the Mantra	28
Found	30
Imprisoned	31
Babylon	33
Anger	35
Valhalla	36
Murder	39
Transgressions	40
Recollections from the Grave	42
Cosmic Fugue	43
Arrogance	45
Arousal	47
Living With a Ghost	48
Consummation	49
The Coming of the Lord	51
Conversations	52
Nadir	54
Alba	55
Terminations	56

Ignominy	58
Culminations	60
The Arrival	61
The Swarm	63
The Ending	74
Epilogue	76

The Tarantella

Akhenaten	79
Intermezzo	80
Nefertiti	81
The Dream	82
Thumbelina	83
Byzantium	84
Dismantling of Stonehenge	86
Scribe	88
Coming Home	89

THE WALTZ

Prologue

Gilgamesh, being of Sumerian descent, has grown tired of his life of luxury and excess in heaven and decides to leave heaven after dreaming about finding a perfect lover. The following pages describe Gilgamesh's attempt to find this lover on Earth and of the people that he meets during his adventures. Gilgamesh is chased by God who is angry that he had the audacity to reject heaven but God cannot navigate the world he created very well and is himself victimized. Gilgamesh seems caught between two worlds, one ancient and archaic where idealism is rampant and a world of civilization and technology; a world that he can only communicate with in dream-like states. Gilgamesh is assisted in his quest for his Mycenaean Queen by the Hunter who rescues him but who is on his own journey to save his wife captured by the Necromancer; by Atropine who was killed in a ritualistic sacrifice but saved by God in order to chase down Gilgamesh; by Valkyrie who seeks absolution from death and defeat in battle; by Odalisque, a former prostitute now stricken with leprosy who longs for a lover from her youth. They are all besieged by Necromancer who captures souls for his own ends and seeks to keep Gilgamesh from finding his perfect lover. In doing so, Gilgamesh would substantiate a life of idolatry that both Necromancer and God require in order to keep the status quo; what are their seats of power.

Gilgamesh:

Summer moon on a rain dance night,
As the young bodies writhe in union;
Noble dragons in a charlatan's parade.
The waters of a pool softly mingle
With each others' scintillating twinkle,
While I sip an archaic pantheon's tea.
Vapors of this herbal sublime brew
Rise and fall like ancient empires,
Long dead kings and war-cloven halls,
Where still some Sirens sadly sing.
And ring, ring, goes the bell calling these
Tempestuous souls away from their play;
And nighttime's sensuous Bacchanal
Has reached the portal of a twilight day.
Now alone I can still envision
The sounds and fleeting glimpses
Of pool bodies and wavy tinkles.
And I feel a yearning deeply spurring
Me to leave this buffered Eden.
Ingesting final vestige of opaque tea,
Sigh and stretch, I tiptoe quietly
Across the pool upon the backs
Of water lilies and lotus leaves.
In distance through the darkness
I hear the Pharaoh start to sing,
Of fairies lounging within the chambers,
Of a six-tiered marble mastaba.
His baleful strains pierce the ebony;
And I cry at thought of lounging fairies.
I've reached the boundaries of Eden,
Across the pool of Utopia's defenses.
Now two-fanged bats with talons,
Appear to saber this incipient soul away.
I've a mission, a goal, a new-found tension;
I've gone to find my Mycenaean Queen,
A princess, an innate, erudite being.

The Flight:

In his flight from Eden Gilgamesh,
Gave up heaven for a garden of Gethsemane;
He took a chance and wagered his soul,
For an ideal and maybe being.
For the world outside was both
Paleolithic and palpably pristine.
Stone-age warriors roamed the plains,
With spears drawn and wild manes;
They preyed upon the un-initiated
And killed with injudicious ferocity.
Feral creatures haunted the nights
And chased the light-time of the days.
Unbidden and unforeseen
They pounced upon and molested
Abused corpses before the dawn.
Many, many, jungles lay in-between;
So the quest and its non-futility,
Lay heavy in the psyche of
This protagonist and would-be king.
Now townships and safe havens,
Lay scattered through the wilderness;
Like distant pearls of mothers,
Villages of people with inns,
Harboring both excesses and sins,
Existed about the forests and within.
It was near one such as this,
That a hunter seeking sustenance,
Saw a sabered Gilgamesh and
Sent a terminal messenger,
A vicious dart into undercarriage
Of said two-fanged carrion.
With a bat-like shriek and sudden start,
Pierced carrion flopped into the dark.
And lo brave Gilgamesh was allowed
His journey's incipient plot,
To become self-evident and bold.
He landed wounded and unwound,

From the talons of the beasts,
Bruised and concussion-ed,
Here, him the hunter found,
Unconscious, lying on the ground.

Mycenaean Queen:

A lilting voice wafted through the air,
Of incense laden, burdened atmosphere;
And aromas from cherry groves have up-risen,
Beyond the crenellation's surrounding walls;
Creating a mélange of olfactory fare.
It is the end of an ancient dusky eve,
When even Sun's rays are slightly soporific,
Making a susurrus miasma of the senses.
And there she sits wearing the cerements
Of a mourning for a love that isn't;
So she sings and she sings and she wishes,
For that someone to answer her missives.
Stone fixtures rove about the garden,
Creating a certain magic mixture;
Steeped with a tincture of the ages.
She's withdrawn to her courtyard that's hidden,
From sight of would-bes and voyeurs,
Who might share in her precious, private tea,
Of aromas and olfactory fares.
While drip go the drops of the tacit tears,
Drops whom she knows as sisters;
They're friends, they're lovers who sift the creases
From off of cheeks so often spent
Fatigued and never fully rested.
But she's wise for her youth,
And she harbors a masonry faith that
Someday soon a lover she will meet;
To transcend hours spent in soliloquy,
To vacillate from joys to pleasures,
To live merrily meandering,

From one coral reef to another,
In an aqueous pageantry,
To the next silky, satin and Sybaritic,
Humbly serene, eidetic scene.
But until this prince shall come,
Alone she must continually gaze,
Across the fields and wooded plains,
Through the cumulus and stately cirrus;
Through the darkness and stormy nimbus.
And in her eyes one can see the clouds,
Sail through in staid formations,
Across an iris in eternal dilation.
One spent in yearning, needful concentration.
Then a sigh, a frown, this princess
Must come down from lofty prisons,
And shrinking castle walls.
The logic, her minds eye reasons,
That she suffers from wishful thinking,
And should give herself to someone else's,
Desirous, clumsy, unpleasant ministrations.
But no! This vision she won't release,
Until her hair is gray, and birds
No longer play;
Until her back is bent, and bats
No longer prey.
This princess will hold on!

Necromancer:

In a cave, a series of grottoes,
Lie sequestered a thousand plundered fairies;
These seraphim, these angelic creatures,
Are preserved in sarcophagi by a master,
Whose spells and charms are meted,
By sordid and fetid, sundry asters.
He poses and wields his magic,
His thaumaturgy and prescience,
In front of a blue-flame, a gaseous chariot;

Which his spirit whips through realms
Of worlds and thoughts unimaginable.
Until his awareness upon a figment perches,
Then the hapless sentient,
Stumbles, lurches and morphoses,
Into the naiad trinkets that are,
This strange warlock's unconscious collection,
Of human fairies and quiet, imprisoned souls.
Souls with only thoughts of manacles
To trust in and to carry.
His neon hair illuminates the cavern,
Where abides his magic chariot; there.
Its violet complexion, of hair
In traipsing locks stumbles suddenly
To shoulders now harnessing hair and its gallop
Of trotting locks and strands.
Reptilian eyes like a newts,
Or chameleons, devoid of iris'
Dividing lines of shade and color,
Drill the center of the pyre,
And cause the consummation of the fire,
To buck, and spark, and holler.
But the refrain of pyre, fire, and holler,
Never, not once, makes his eyes to wander.
His skin, like his eyes, no color,
Paler even than a midday pond of water,
Captures his features, seemingly put there,
By a demented and manic nighttime sculptor.
A pendulous, chartreuse robe, almost tapestry,
Spun by Clothos in all her artistry,
Rotors around his person,
Like the creeping tendrils of a lambent,
Iridescent and tundra form of lichen.
And so this Hadean monarch;
This pernicious, fallow Mephistopheles
Counts his trinkets, and this night,
As every one before, snaps his fingers,
And now there's a thousand and one,
Suspended, and sad midnight fairies.
   And somewhere out in the night,
A solitary figure dreams of horrid bats,
Clawing at his dreamy reverie.

He awakens and from his bosom there
Is missing, a certain love or passion.
That he harbored like a trove, a
Treasure chest that was wife and lover.
He was in the foliage hunting,
And woke at night torn asunder;
Knowing that the thunder and the clapping,
Signaled the kidnaping of his
Mate and soul of souls.
Now from this night his mission was adopted,
To seek her visage-and-the vengeance,
Upon the thief-and-the taker.

The Sacrifice:

       Volcanic eruptions inundate the wasteland,
Ash sprinkles the lava flows,
Bringing once proud conifers to their knees.
Dark stratus is sucked to the sphincter
Of volcano and its core;
Seemingly like a magnet, attracting metal
Drones and bits of steel.
One can see the glow of molten magma's
Mixture creeping still below the ground;
And eldritch vapors exude themselves
All around somewhat like,
Vapor warriors undulating in an eerie,
Tribal combative dance.
And seeping over this pyroclastic covered surface
Of patinas and strange hues;
There is a band of people
Struggling to the edge of cone.
Now in strange gyrations these supplicants,
Raise a girl whose all upbound,
To the rocky throne,
And keep her there imprisoned,

By a pole, a rope and a noose.
Then they run, they flee, they escape,
To nadir of erupting dome;
Leaving the girl there, bound and all alone.
Time for her beats with the ejected molten,
And she knows that for her time is a paucity;
A drying font, and empty bowl;
A clock with one hand missing.
And so this inverted, proud Prometheus,
Shudders at first touch of liquid stone;
Volcanic vultures burn her to the bone.
Her eyes in agony gaze upward
To an errant clap of thunder.
It strikes and steals her soul,
Tearing asunder her body from the pole--
So in the end she dies but not alone.

The Awakening:

When my ghost got up and shuddered,
I screamed down and barely uttered,
A dilapidated, vocal dry-heave.
Mouth with liquid was not sated,
Parched like a sun-drenched beach,
Or salt flats that have been bleached;
I could barely breathe.
My mind escaped the unholy torture,
Of a fall from purity to cant;
I can't, can't, believe this dilemma,
Or interpret the conflicting emotions.
I want, I need, I desire;
Therefore I am higher, ascendant;
Or maybe just lower.
Half I am and learning still, to
Shed this snake's skin and molt my will;
I perceive a mountain with an Indian name,

How I know, I know not,
But I am not me and feel so caught,
By the vicissitudes of another's confounding
And unpleasant drownings in a vacuous,
Sea or ocean of inner commotion.
I see a peak and wish there to climb;
I soon get there and then feel fine;
Gazing out over a valley on verge of eve;
There's a city with myriad lights beckoning me.
I know the place, but have never seen it,
It doesn't make sense or even
Fit into that thing called experience.
There's someone down there I feel akin to,
And someone over the peak that I yearn for.
Crawling up through layers of pain,
I shed the shackles that have maimed
Limbs, brain and coronary meter.
Now on me there is a light,
As of sun's rays, just as bright.
Coaxing eyelids open that in a coma have been,
Is a tedium I don't want to do again.
But I did.
I see a stranger who is seeing me,
But do not feel a fright or a danger.
Intuitively I soon guess,
This man in his hunter's dress,
Is my finder and arbalest savior.
In another world I've been a-sleeping,
If you'll excuse me--I've been a-dreaming.

Atropine:

Left to die an ignoble sacrifice
This girl did die but as said before,
But once again, not alone.
For in the end God did save her,

And spirited her lamenting soul away.
But not without a reason, or a goal,
Or a price, or an ineffable rhyme.
All sanctuaries do contain a price,
Even those instilled by heaven
And vicars on earth thereof.
So she became an angel surreal
And winged with haloed diadem;
A prelate to contest the vagrancies
Of evil souls on earth.
      Shrouded in mystic, niveous satin,
She carouses with the heavens,
And caresses the unleavened vistas,
With a new-found air of freedom,
And profound sense of catharsis.
But her mission calls and perforce she
A deity to you and me must
Answer the musings of stringent duty.
Eyes sooty from recent epiphany;
The dawning of dying to be reborn,
And realizations of God's calling.
She's not what she was before,
And ware the demon's kiss that
Is the nemesis and angel's death
In Wizard's form in earthen throne;
He is the enemy within.
Assiduous with seraph's knowledge,
And now an armed celestial being,
Bearing Zues' mighty thunderbolt,
Atropine responds to the summons,
And the dearth of a good on earth.
She departs to seek out Gilgamesh.

God's Ire:

    No more sirens sadly sing, and
The Mastabas have all fallen down;
Instead now in the distance

Cromlechs march to a far off beat,
And sandaled feet of enslaved souls
Line up to enter within them.
A flying buttress to uphold heaven,
Now spans the gap between it;
Of earth and that abandoned Eden
That Gilgamesh chose to leave.
For when a God exits Sangri-la
In pursuit of a love that isn't,
He disrupts the synchronicity of life,
For immortals and their sentient flocks.
The angels flutter useless wings,
Like beings no longer virile,
And their haloes fall two inches shorter,
So that purity seems a little smaller;
The waters quit their twinkling,
Their magical, musical, dulcet tinkling;
Now slosh like a cesspool's gaseous tide.
And God did get angry at
The presumptions of a fleeing Gilgamesh.
Who so upset the fluid balance
Of idols sitting in the scales,
And floating in happy, sedated trances;
That he retrieved a messenger who
Had been mortal unto death;
Now, having never been to heaven,
She, an entry-level spirit,
This moribund, volcanic sprite,
Was free to roam said hills and dales
Of a constricted, typhoid earth.
To seek out him who denied both Eden
And indirectly slapped the face of God,
For the frailty of an earth-bound lover.
As if the sex of heaven,
Was the kiss of treason,
And the pleasures of a God only
Dandelions dangling in a field of weeds.

Late Night Dream:

      In a dream, a miasmic scheme,
It came to her one lonely night;
The birds were all asleep beyond the
Open balcony's double doors.
A pleasant breeze chose to waft,
And soft, softly, waltzed into the room,
Where desolate princess caressed the matt,
Embraced the pillow, and loved the blanket,
Which embraced her lovingly back.
Her wayward strands of hair,
Fluttered beyond the confines of the bed,
So long it was they water-fell,
Over the mattress edge.
The starlight that patted in,
Silent as a cat's paw, just as dim,
Sought safe haven and a harbor,
Amongst the tresses of said princess.
So that when this breeze came in,
It stirred the star flakes into
A subtle orbit about her face.
So that nothing was as beautiful
In the human race as princess was
That serene and storied night,
Of sneaky zephyr and starlight.
      But in the reverie that came over
Her amongst the dew-drops of sleepy,
Sundry, and steamy wishful thinking,
She saw a God escape from heaven,
And never, even, ever return again.
What a glorious figure this traipsing,
Lonesome, sculpture was in running,
From something all mortals thought perfect.
He was the one that she sought,
The one for whom she so resolutely waited,
And dreamed of all the time;
Somewhere out in the night he rested,
A mere mortal now, not as godly,
With imperfection though, he got better;
Unfettered by the manacles of heaven.

And she did love him like no timid
Soul before or myriad, many other.
The passion waned and starlight thinned;
Matutinal rays coalesced,
As the morning vapors transgressed
The portal balcony doors;
Causing a chill to fill the air.
Sweet princess curled, began a shudder,
From the precipitation in atmosphere.
Her eyelids fluttered and like
A doe or fawn so freshly born,
Warm, and newly thrown from the womb,
She gazed around at a strange
Or foreign, wondrous new world.
Where birds always awakened--singing;
Sun's rays bright and polar,
Created a visual cacophony,
Of altisonant, luminated particles,
Glissading in and out of separate sunbeams.
So she, with hope, awoke the morning
After related latter dream,
Thinking that, perhaps after all,
It wasn't just a doleful schema,
Or that woeful, woeful,
--Wishful thinking

Temptation:

There she was dancing amongst the flowers,
A tree nymph flying with the honeybees,
Pollinating Helio theistic and wild rose-buds;
It was an incredible pristine frieze,
Not frozen though, as she leaped a bowing
Genuflecting and fallen tree branch.
Even the thorns turned their poignant,
Honed, and sharpened heads,
In honor of this prancing sprite,

With long hair held by breeze,
Always three steps behind her.
Dragonflies meandered around this waif;
An entourage of a debutante that will forever
Remain in her coming out.
And honey suckles toss themselves from
Their ascending, intertwined tree vines;
That like nature's Babel must attempt to climb,
From tree vine to heaven's ambrosia wine;
To disseminate their perfume musk,
Along the path of dancing, female Pan.
      This was the vision that assaulted the
Weary senses of Hunter and nomad Gilgamesh.
They came across the path and drank the aroma
In strange libation to the beauty they saw.
To catch this nymph and give their love,
Was all they both could surmise;
For no sunrise would ever be so bright,
Or dusk ever so restful or relaxing,
Or twilight so blue or comforting,
As they would be with the sprite;
That spirit-nymph who was running out of sight.
And in the back of minds, they
Could not believe how easily resolve
And lover's single-minded mission
Took to flight, a gazelle in the Serengeti
Fleeing the condition of an inflamed lion,
Or a shifting dune of the Sahara,
Always just a moment's step ahead
Of the impassioned, hunting gust.
But a different passion overtook them and they too,
Began to run and to give a-chase;
In search of love, with complete abandon;
Nothing else matters!

Evil's Journey:

      Riding the moon's a skill Necromancer,
In all his glory and narcissism, never tired of;
He was a screaming banshee upon a glowing orb,

And a wayward wizard who waned and grew;
With the flick of his wand, he was something more.
But this convoluted Phaethon who did
Nothing else nor drive the sun,
Only rode the moon when there
Was something he should see.
When the lightening took the vision of
His servants and loyal bats;
Who had been bringing him an even
Better prize than a sleeping naiad,
Something was grossly amiss,
And he didn't know what it was.
But this Mephistophelian sensed that
God in heaven was not at ease
With that something that he could not see,
A tension bathed the very air,
And the shrill cry of his dying bats
Reverberated still against his will,
And nothing would ever change it.
       Alighting in a field of mushrooms,
Magician, moon and magic came to earth;
And in the dearth of sunlight,
Felt around the world.
Seeking for the one thing or several
That made the one God sing in anger;
And shatter the antimony
That was the alloy of earth and heaven.
So Magician, moon and magic held hands
And partook of the mushrooms;
They saw all, beheld more, and lived
At least a thousand lifetimes within
The altered confines of halcyon,
Hallucinogenic and dreamy leas.
And the Magician made love to the lune.
And in orgasmic prescience viewed,
Through climactic, cosmic copulation;
Sorcerer with glee witnessed the fleeing
Of lonely Gilgamesh on his solemn,
Solitary, and now wanton hegira.
Upon the moon, with rotor-ing robe,
Magician fled now home.
What would be his next act,

What would be a thoughtful step?
Were the convolutions of his mind.
One thing that was certain,
Was Gilgamesh must never attain,
The thought or flesh of a fluid lover,
And on earth must always now remain.
Necromancer, in his room of fairies,
Certainly had room for more.

Valkyrie:

     Valkyrie rises above the frozen plain
Of tundra wasteland where before,
A thousand hunting warriors raced
Into the phalanx of a battle's maw.
She scans the horizon that's a bleeding,
Pinioned and supine soldier's corpse;
His arms hang towards the earth,
And his chest heaves up to the sun;
A dusk born in a horrid agony;
A spear impales his bucking chest.
She turns from this tortured image
Of death and war and pestilence;
While three armored horsemen trot across
The bloodied, hemophelia-ed heavens.
Anger bursts her hauberk, bearing
Her own glorious and heaving breasts.
She draws her sword suspended in the sky,
As the ire-sweat glistens and shines
Upon a forehead furrowed with strange
Lines and eerie, eldritch signs.
This Goddess will give holy chase
To horsemen and their avocations.
Dying men and unnatural bodies,
Cry out to Valkyrie for her to revenge.
Argent hair coruscates and sparkles,

With the static of her soon vengeance;
She sets herself to the godly race.
Muscles stiffen, her belly moistens;
Such beauty in her chiseled face.
But the set leaves her jaw,
And those lovely breasts, the air from which,
Suddenly, silently begins to evacuate.
Her toned muscles slacken;
Her argent hair now flaxen.
The falchion tip drops from heaven.
Wild Asgaard calls her home;
Those horsemen she cannot beat,
Not but though a hundred men she could
Defeat without a flicker or a thought
To their finesse or fighting prowess.
But those horsemen she cannot meet;
For she too suffers only fate;
Something Gods must wrestle with,
Though not always happy with.
Sweet Valkyrie bows her noble visage,
Turns her back and kneels,
Her eyes close; A tear.
Slowly off her cheek it tumbles;
And down on earth,
The snow, in eider tufts,
--It comes..........

Odalisque:

In the southern Negev, where
The air is warm or rather hot,
Haunts a colony of lepers,
Clothed in scant robes and shreds
Of garments as they weren't supposed
To be before they were forced to flee,
The company of reflecting society.
Limbs now stumps wave about,
Like seaweed in a gently ebbing sea;
They can't manipulate the environment,

So they pat the backs and other lumps
Of humans melting in the glare,
Of an unimpeded desert sun,
Above a hellish, and heinous habitat.
   And there is a girl who sits
Alone in a cave as she cries and heaves,
With sobs that cannot purge themselves
Of the pain of the reality that is.
A shadur veil hides the gaping
Gangrenous flesh that was
A nose upon an erupting face.
Opaque eyes wander listlessly
Seeking one last image; uselessly.
The agony of her lament,
Crawls around the spider's web
Of cave, cavern and residence.
She cannot comprehend what became
Of her inchoate coquette life;
Where her eyes could make a man
A boy, and a boy a man; or
Even a celibate monk a failure.
She kneels over, a genuflection to a dream.
   A dancing girl, a swaying harlot,
A slut in a menagerie;
She had the men heavily breathing.
Not a noble avocation or a
Parent's wish for a child's virtuosity;
To be meted out for money;
Virginity spent economically.
But she made her own way and loved,
Even if just once.
But she lived, hugged and was held,
Even if it was not still.
After a night of dancing for the brothel Queen,
Odalisque fell to the embrace
Of her simple handsome lover.
He excused her previous others;
And caressed her breast; for he loved her.
He tastes her mascaraed tears,
And sheds a few of his own.
Together they susurrate, they mingle,
Beneath a feathered quilt,

Where they've built a holy temple;
There, worship is simple, and
The touch is another treasure.
      It's just a memory pleasure;
Satori in a dream scape,
Where the craters are the pitfalls,
And recollections are sensations, that
The body can no longer feel or sensate.
Masturbation's become an empty gesture;
A cup of briny water,
In a stagnate, stench infested
Swamp of mosquito ridden pustules.
The surface of memories lies green and alga-ed;
She's awakened.
She knows she can't go on,
Like this, she's become an embittered,
Fettered, and unsettled soul.
She unveils her imprisoned
Pouch of biding Bella Donna.
Bit by bit she consumes the lot,
From her trusty hidden pot,
That carried her mortal concoction
From its hiding to savoring palate;
And so she passes from earth;
With her sobs and shudders,
Suddenly just slightly louder.
And her tears and features,
In a death mutate faster,
to become in the idleness,
That much better.

Questions:

      And I love her, the girl I
Espied from behind the door;
The coy glances, the open smile,
Her radiant hair, and fixture
Of a statue that shadows
My haunted soul.
I didn't think that a God could lust;

Maybe only a running nymph,
Or secret Calypso,
That on an island doth sit,
And awaits a stranded stranger,
To float upon her sandy shore.
These are the pictures
That I conjured while racing
Through the forest and Soylent green,
Of fauna that separates
Body, mind and being.
But I do lust.
And I believe that I lust for her.
Am I only dreaming
Of a sea-maiden in a shell,
Who with a bell is ringing
That elusive toll of feeling,
Which gongs so seldomly,
Or oft rarely, with
Sound and introduction shrilly? Yes,
I do lust.
With a faith that some
Would probably call unseeing,
Purblind or glacoma-ed.
   But the door slams shut;
I must be dreaming,
For I am moving,
And after her a-running;
Some strange maiden, or siren
Who with limbs and aroma,
Lithely, lissomly is wailing;
While Hunter and I march into
the clutches of that Scylla or
Ancient coral-colored Charybdis.
I must awake from hypnosis,
For a God can only be,
Free and healthy, wholesome,
If he suffers not the trances
Of an enticing female person
Who isn't his one and only,
Or mate and soul of souls.
   Gilgamesh awakens and
Knows he should not be a-running

For that pseudo,
Shapely, feeling
Of a girl
That's full of guile;
Of a waif
That's coy and wile.

The Dream:

      I've no more faith in your empty promises,
Or belief in your phony convictions;
For while you told me of faithfulness,
You whispered in the ear of faithlessness.
For you infidelity was raised supreme,
And other men placed as kings.
You romped in the fields of dandelions,
And chased not the happy butterflies,
But caroused in the taverns and inns,
With rose-bearing phony Romeos.
Your "last" said he was not the first, but
The final bead on a bleeding,
Broken and stained rosary.
You've tainted the cross of our love,
And lost the value in memories.
Now when I think of you I cringe,
Because other men have been,
Where before only I had been.
For you love was spelled a lie, and
Honesty half and three-quarter truths.
You gave freely what once was special,
And tainted your soul with mud.
      But the dandelions can change,
To blooming, vibrant violets;
And the letters of lie can be erased.
You don't need to whisper in the ear,
Of faithlessness and infidelity; But

Should now yell to the sun,
And shed tears for the betrayal you've done.
You can promise to me a life-time,
And grant our love repatriation.
Our caresses can come from exile,
On Calypso's lonesome isle.
The string of rosary can be mended,
And the beads bleached and prayed again.
The cross of our love can pendulum,
Off devotion's courtly commingle.
But it will take some dedication,
For you to color my faded trust.
But you must never lie again,
To me or with a shallow other.
Darling-you can make us better.
      The girl across the Indian mountain,
Whereupon I had been yearning,
Told me a tale of retribution,
That she did to me sometime ago,
For transgressions to her which,
I must once have committed.
But I knew I had atoned,
For those distant, hazy sins.
Still, she went on with the tale,
And the agony of what she inflicted,
Caused my chest to start a-hurting,
And my face to start convulsing,
In tortured grimaces of woeful,
Painful, wistful weeping.
      All I now remember,
Is that we were in the sylvan a-running,
Ruing the elusiveness of love.
I and the Hunter were a-chasing;
Enamored by a transient sprite.
Somehow we landed in this valley,
Unconscious and asleep.
If you'll excuse me,
For once and again,
I must have been a-dreaming.

Forgive:

Nailed to a cross, my wrists are bleeding,
My feet hurt and my head is pounding;
I can't breathe.
I look down and see your face,
It's so wonderful, childish, crying.
Through my pain I sense your anguish,
And know you don't mean this.
You pound another nail; a blow.
I'm buffeted by agony, it hurts;
Begging for mercy, I'm pleading.
Your tears enrapture, enthrall me, as
I join them stumbling off your visage.
I can't scream;
Please don't leave me!
Wishing for an end to torment,
I desire the spear of Longinus,
Receiving instead the lance of a glare;
I can't stand it!
Piercing chest, between the ribs,
But please leave my heart intact.
Twist the tip, and turn the edges,
But please don't take your love back.
Overcome now you fall to your knees,
And moan that you love me.
"I know" I say,
"You don't mean this."
I toss my hair and splinters enter spine,
I no longer feel them.
My love of loves is
There before me and
It comforts me to hear your lamenting.
It's almost over, I am ended;
No more nails can hold me, or spear
Forever pinion or impale me.
I'm no longer inhaling;
But with last breath,
Your adoration doesn't flee or fail me;
Rather it supports me.
I touch your crown and stroke your hair,

God, I love you!
The nails have vanished, my ribs no scar,
The blood has dried and I espy a star;
It dawdles in the heavens,
Right by Neptune or planet Venus.
I pick you up from off your knees,
Kiss your forehead and on you breathe.
Your eyes no more hard or brittle,
Like frail or fallow diamonds;
But lithe and supple; endearing.
Binary suns with eyelids caressing,
Creating with each and every blink,
A solar, happy, summer's day, and
Dusky, dormant, haven night.
Slowly, tightly, we embrace;
I whisper to you, "It's okay,"
Uttering softly I say,
-- "I forgive you."

Back To the Mantra:

     It's back to the Mantra, back
To being alone and lonely;
To the empty chantings of "I love you."
Those evil hisses issue forth,
From Sorceress' lips they kiss my
Forehead in an evil curse and touch,
Of a branded T for thief and taker.
     God discovered my soul in hiding,
Amongst the thrushes and bulrushes
Of empty hope and dreams of folly.
Whilst visions passed free and willing,
When upon his entry I sat screaming,
For all my dreams were slowly
Ripped ceremoniously from me.
     It's back to the Mantra,

In heaven I once orated,
The ineffable portents of power,
That in Eden was just a prison,
And desires changed quickly like a
Prism in a raindrop falling,
In springtime's runoff cataract.
      How was I found out, how
In the world did the devil deceive;
How in the world could I have believed?
At least place a noose about
My strung and broken neck,
To justify and somehow explain,
A found soul that was well-hidden.
      Back to the Mantra in heaven,
Where dancing fairies are now crippled,
And shriven with sneers upon their faces.
Water lilies sink in ponds of oil;
And the black stuff weighs a spirit,
Unused to the toil of disillusionment;
I can't live here anymore!
      It must be the pain of knowing,
The torture of can't be a-running,
And the thought of empty Mantras,
Inhabiting dry, and tepid Saharas.
That is the climate of my mind; and,
The wasteland of my shredded being;
The semblance of being struck.
      And now no God, but only,
The venom of dripping spiders,
Playing on their webs of reasons,
Clutching at captured, silken Mantras;
So I cry and weep against the treason;
Back to the Mantra I unfold:
"Oh please God, not again!"

Found:

       Chanting monastic, polytonal phrases;
"I saved you from the dead,"
Said this neo-natal Hera,
Proud of a new-found omnipotence.
"I am Atropine, created through the need,
Of an irate over-lord in heaven;
To retrieve the God who vomited
The Ambrosia and the Manna
Of the honey-dew laden chambers of Nirvana.
You're not to ever leave again, once
In heaven you've been re-deposited."
The granite of her voice was though
Betrayed by the feather of her stare;
And compassion overcame her
For the state of Gilgamesh and the Hunter.
That state of a wounded mare in a coma,
Unable to save her dying foal
Trapped in a tar prison or bitumen pit.
Looking at Gilgamesh--
"Why did you ever leave?"
"I left for the lack of a lover;
In Nirvana loneliness was the death touch,
Satan's grip around a worthless treasure."
"But all of heaven is a mess,
Cherubs horde the clouds; they're crass,
And apostles' chalices are filled last.
And God now charges golden doubloons
For a flask of the cheapest Chardonnay;
And Judas--he's been forgiven to collect
An oenophiles luxury tax."
       The birds of paradise have all milked
The honey-dew of a misbegotten heaven.
That ideal that Gilgamesh wanted to
Extrapolate from an earth-bound lover,
Has come crashing down around his head;
And Hunter can no longer espy his other;
That significant wholesome pleasure,
That was both wife and mother.
       Magician, sorcerer, or the opposite that

Exists in all of us: that Necromancer
Has corrupted the visions of Knights-errant.
Their images, their ideals have turned
Against them--traitors to a cause,
That in beginning was so promising.
In their minds where once these ideals
Roamed freely, there haunts only ghosts;
Pangs of thoughts that could have been.
Negatives of pictures they should have seen.
Now in minds eye only vapid silence where
Once the rustling of romantic measures,
Slid up and down mental balustrades.
Now in gray matter only hollow chasms where
Once the echoes of joyful laughter,
Reverberated across make-believe buttresses;
Their phantasies were ripped slowly from them;
Their purity left stained and broken;
Their dreams and desires turned poltergeists,
Screaming in the night.

Imprisoned:

    Lying there scheming, I realized
That, still again, I must have been a-dreaming:
    It was that verdant world, a greenery,
Where all the oxygen is pearls, and
Clergy are Gods among men.
Sensing a city, a place replete with pity,
With the image of my sultry lover;
One who has caused my mission,
To mutate into a pang of treason,
Thereby altering the course
Of our fated, mis-begotten idolatry.
That perfumed human carnage
Meant to be my bride and treasure,
Has left the music measure sad and empty.
I search this place and yes she's gone;

The Jordan river seems so long,
And lotus leaves have supplanted, by
Virtue of their sunny, semen laden reflection,
The green of the copper ridden stream.
The paths and trails of this mnemonic place,
Hardly seem the same, and
The shame of my crawling still
Scavenges around the refuse piles
With the magpies and the sputtering vermin.
Yes she is and always will be--gone.
      Snapping back I feel the slapping
Of callous hands about my cheek and brow.
"Are you a God or mendicant,
Which I cannot tell?"
"I'm both and neither and you'd do well,
To avoid this cursed wretch."
My co-prisoner in this cave of ice,
Held herself secluded behind a veil
Whose tatters whispered of her life;
Betraying toil and emotional strife.
As a God I could verily sense; taste even
The gangrenous breath and pestilence,
Of a leper manacled by disease.
She must have felt my perspicacious touch,
Pulling away with her soylent green.
"It's okay, as a deity I'm immune,
And as a wretch I'm just like you."
"I knew you were a God, you're Delphic,
You're an oracle drinking the wine of heaven.
But you must have made the one God angry,
To strap you in a cell with a leper;
For here in this cave the air and light are Trappist
Monks who chant in elemental tones."
"Yes, the one God with me was irate,
For I made a date with a schema;
A dream of a wife and a lover,
Not found in the trances of Nirvana.
I sought the embraces of an earth-bound lover,
And instead he's awarded me the timid
Tendrils of a cave-bound leper.
Justice is a heady drink."

Babylon:

      Six years passed with Princess still as pretty,
On this night as the first when then she
Dreamed of her traipsing God;
But no savior ever has come
Through the portal of her bedroom door,
No messiah ever tiptoed across the tapestry
Lining the carpentry of her chamber floor.
No wondrous, loving significant other
To elope on a wedding with,
To make love with on a summer's eve.
"Where, oh where could he be,
This God who would not abandon me?"
Princess died some two thousand deaths;
One for each night she's went to bed alone
During the six year interim of dreaming God,
And the present where she dies once again.
She can't go on like this, she's
Kept the faith and fought the others,
Who with her wished to be.
Everyone thought her mad, and
Considered the garden where she roamed,
The walls of her prison cell.
While the midnight moon held its sway,
The gardener wondered where she went in circles
Around the Acacia and exotic shrubs.
Who she talked to, pleaded with,
Until her eyes grew heavy-ish;
And she'd lay down, not from fear, but
The fatigue of crying or begging for
Whoever it was waiting beyond the mantle
Of chamber, castle, or kingdom door.
Once asleep, the gardener, as before, would
Pull the vines and crawling ivy
About her person to keep her warm.
And when she lay there thus ensconced,
She appeared a Druid Queen,
Enveloped by the supplicants
Who worshiped this heavenly being.
What a beautiful scene, this woody, natural thing:

Gardener, vines, and Queen;
Moonlight, madness, and faithfulness;
Among the castle's crenellations,
Protecting the boundaries of Babylon,
And preserving the purity in her love.
And along the paths of the garden
Where she chose to tread and
Her tiptoes met the ground;
The Hyacinth, the Rosebuds, the Rhodora,
All grew wild, and much prettier; higher,
Than where those sanguine steps
Were never felt nor found.
Perhaps it was her teardrops
That tinkled; little glass crystals,
That sprinkled where she walked.
Princess was in pain,
For if no God ever came,
Would she ever love again?
So she sleeps, and she sleeps, and she's wishful;
But her trance isn't unlike a coma,
And the wishing is a little doubtful;
It's been six years of waiting
For that special, dreamy lover,
The knightly missioned savior.
      A sudden gust of chill air,
Brushes the flora and the fauna
Of the garden and the gardener.
And so deep was "she" asleep, the
Frost on her face couldn't wake her.
And Necromancer who rode the moon,
Stepped down into this nursery,
Crushing the hibiscus and the tulips.
He didn't care; for only one plant
Did he even wonder where.
His newt-like eyes espied the princess,
Though the plants and vines pulled tighter;
Valiantly they tried to hide her.
So from his fingers he sent some lasers,
Scorching the vines and ivy to the root.
The whole garden shuddered,
And a single, simple cry was uttered,
Waking the gardener from his sopor.

Seeing Magician with his treasure,
What we would call a prisoner,
The gardener attacked him.
        In the morning it was found
That the garden had been ravished;
And the gardener sadly crucified.
His blood, like an alpine rill,
Trickling still down the Acacia.
The pond it made upon the ground,
Had mixed with the charred and broken ivy.
But a shape like an arrow could be seen,
Betwixt the mixture of blood and vines,
Pointing directly to the east.
Then it was discovered that someone
With the princess had absconded.
And the import of that arrow;
That last daring act of man and garden,
Now was known--
The invader lived beneath the rising sun,
Flying only in the darkness of the night;
And he'd ripped the heart from the kingdom,
And shredded the breast of Babylon.

Anger:

      So the Hunter now was wakened,
From his nap he was risen, and
He knew that things were somewhat different,
Than when he was a friend for a God.
"I guess no mission was too sacred,
Or holy quest too precious or dear
To be forsaken; forgotten, or even taken."
Innately he knew the one God with Gilgamesh
Was still angry;
He knew the one God was at the meeting
When Atropine came with the summons;

That sacrosanct and holy fiat,
That papal burden for to prison,
A fleeing God who only wanted to find a living,
With a certain someone like who the Hunter
Was seeking; searching.
       He got up from off the ground and
Glanced unsurely at his surroundings.
The trees, the bushes, the grassy vistas;
The flowers, the fruit, and the berries,
Only gave him pangs of guilt;
Only filled him full of silt.
Then the storm clouds came, thus en-framing
The rollicking hills off in the distance;
Where the mountains began off to the east,
He knew t'was there where wife and lover
Lay so sadly conscious un-encumbered.
But now he had two missions to complete:
Gilgamesh the God was his friend and
He'd never let him lie imprisoned;
He'd never let him lie emblazoned,
With the ignominy of a God un-treasured.
So with the gallant clop of a war-horse
Left unfettered;
The gallant trot of a knightly steed
Left untethered,
He walked off into the distance,
To find first that wife and lover,
Then free that godly pariah;
These were the tenets of his mind,
They were to him convictions quite divine.

Valhalla:

      Thor and Odin drink and have drunk
To the point of a drunken stupor;
Hammer and lightening are parked there,
Stuck off in the corner.

The saliva drips off of bleeding lips,
For father and son have fought the other,
And as usual there is no winner.
For Gods cannot duel with, or
Banish, one another without the scepter of a reason.
And sweet Valkyrie lies awakened;
She still suffers the sadness of not saving;
She's broken.
Never did she think that
Her back in vainglory would soon sink
Below that horizon,
That far off coast that commingled
With the shimmering demons
Of Aurora Borealis;
That in defeat she would slink
Back to the halls of Valhalla
Where the ghosts of revelry roam.
Now; at this minute,
Odin suffers a broken vision,
That only an intoxicated divinity
Could muster through his vomit.
"Sweet Valkyrie, I know you're broken,
But as I've said you're not perfect,
Though a Goddess you always were.
Those three you could not beat;
That was seen in the stones
That the warriors tossed
On the dawn of that destructive day,
When first you tempted to change the fray.
But I sense that there is a purpose,
A quest that you should impose
Upon yourself to release you from this state.
There is a God whose hour of need
Is now, or never, or all for naught.
He is in a cave, bound and caught;
A porpoise in a tidal pool,
Where death is a minute away.
The one God with him is so angry,
And I fear that Gilgamesh is no longer sanguine.
As children of heaven,
My heart bleeds to see him so."
"Yes father, him I will to aid,

Though a better mistress than I
He should have at this mirthless hour;
I suffer from a broken back,
And fear I lack the strength to persevere.
I see his dilemma in my mind,
It is an image in my heart that pines
For the glory of a vanquished God;
In him I feel I can confide."
"But first dear maiden, daughter of my life,
You must seek the Hunter who seeks his wife.
You must perforce help this mortal
Who suffers only passion for Gilgamesh,
And a wife and lover who establish,
The funeral dirge in another cave,
Of an evil fiend known as Necromancer.
Together you will battle this sorcerer,
Attempt to overcome this pleasurer,
Reveling in the souls of fairies and lovers,
Who bed with him unwillingly."
"Then after this war, this battle with
This warlock who harbors the vanities,
Of druid fairies and woody queens,
We will seek out that noble Gilgamesh?"
"Yes. He will be next on your list.
But ware the one God who lies so angered,
Don't let him see the freedom you attempt to tender.
I'm not sure that's a wrath contained
With my will that's so un-refrained,
Through the coursing of the wines
That in my veins flow so rapidly; I'm a drunk."
So sweet Valkyrie rises yet again,
Inflamed she is to free Gilgamesh;
To find the Hunter and to slay,
That most melancholy of Magicians.
This battle she will not forfeit;
This war she will not counterfeit;
This time she will not yield to it;
What we call--Abandonment.

Murder.

      Too many times the clouds came,
The showers poured and the lightening
Split the thundering storms.
Too long was Gilgamesh locked in that
Subterane, desolate pity;
Where a leper was his only mistress;
And dank stone a bed of bile,
That he couldn't eschew much longer.
Finally his tears came and hope flung
Itself, like a wave upon the shore,
Into the cavern of his empty chest.
Reverberations of its battering
Repeated in loose echolalia,
The phrases of a soul in heat,
With only a broken carcass at its
Feet; the bones left dry and unsated.
And "she" perceived this misery that
Enveloped this once galloping God;
This miscreant Idol whose regal
Carriage was unseated.
She felt the un-whispered reason;
How the treason had left a black hole
Somewhere in the confines of his corse.
It was a chasm she could
'nt fill, it was a sickness that
No cure could ever heal or
A shame no forgiveness would ever
Crawl with at the foot of holy atonement.
He lacked that fluid lover, and this
Bastille otherwise known as cavern,
Only impressed the shadow of the
Vacuum of his center into the fabric
That was Id, Psyche, and godly Hubris.
--Gilgamesh was dying.
      And in his dream Gilgamesh spied
The pinioned, or manacled Prometheus.
How he envied this God his torment,
And physical pain; something he would
Gladly have exchanged

For the mental anguish
Enchaining his emotional whirls,
And the moire tapping at the walls of
Blackhole schism caught within his chest.
And Gilgamesh wondered if indeed,
He died would he secure safe passage
Back to sultry heaven, or
Spend his time chipping at the ice
Of frigid hell?
How would the one God react to his
Dying? How would the one God
Reconcile a deity suffering the fate,
When fate was merely a vessel
Sailing in the corked up bottle
That was heaven?
He'd probably say good riddance.
    And she knew the time was now at hand;
That pragmatism now in cavern;
This cover over the soul of God,
Was at an end.
That the one God had committed sin,
That transgressions were the catch
Words of an oblique day.
For Gilgamesh slowly passed away;
And the one God had indirectly,
But irrevocably,
--Slowly slaughtered him.

Transgressions:

    Here at the feet of an Egyptian land
Encroached the Hunter and his friend.
Valkyrie flew him upon her back,
Deep into the land of Theban thoughts,
Where Nubian slaves danced and beat
On war drums held in awe.
Their feathered heads were fine;
Replete with the ornamentation

Of warriors thus ensconced
In the bridals of their loss.
Egyptians walked their funny feet,
Past a Nile lined with reeds.
Plumed tips undulating with
The breeze, and poor men wandered
Here, sent to harvest them.
And in the river swam the fish-es,
That fed this archaic land.
Rafts that of papyri were constructed,
Darted like blue herons lithely to and fro;
A pungent form of littoral.
      And in the streets and in the pubs
Where beer was served and ladled;
A laughing crowd, the smoky din;
The room was filled with musky air,
And bar-girls roamed the tables.
      Hunter, with Valkyrie,
Appeared in the world of men;
She as both woman and companion.
They needed a clue of "him."
Just a word or a whisper or
A hint of Magician and his den.
That arachnid's claw that near to here,
Lay quietly so well hidden.
So they drank and they drank, and
Valkyrie thus imbibed revealed to
Hunter the secrets of her soul.
The pieces of the puzzle of nebula,
And why not pregnant she lactated;
The nectar of which was radioactive.
They chuckled and teared for so long they feared
That always they would be alone.
For a God on earth to alcohol was
Not unfeeling or un-immune;
So in the end they became amused.
And the others in the misty room,
Lusted after sweet Valkyrie, for
She was as wonderful as a violet
Growing wild on the wilderness of the moon.
But when these two stood,
Inebriated though they were;

The Hunter in his hunter's dress,
Deadly with his arbalest;
And Valkyrie potent as a Goddess;
Discouraged any form of inquiry.
Libidos of the drunkards
Aspiring to what would be rapers,
Didn't dare to impose their wills
Upon the vengeance of these two.
Off they went, hand in hand, to assume
Some privacy and a room where,
They could be alone.
    There the Hunter left his fidelity twined
Among the argent tresses of Valkyrie's hair;
And she her immortality wavering
Between the Hunter and his lair.
They both needed the comforting
Of a salient meeting in a bed.
Now in the morning Hunter's heart was
Reminiscent of, or even felt like lead.
And Valkyrie oh so woeful for losing
The prospect of being never dead.
For when a God inhales a mortal's seed,
They lose the propensity for age infinity.
So now they were as brother-sister,
Companions more than ever;
They were saved by sex,
And bound by the--
Chain-y links of sin.

Recollections from the Grave:

I like it when the leaves fall;
They're ochre, they're rustic,
Reminding one of memories stored in leather.

From off the pages of our Khama Sutra,
Where pages fold and the corners bend,
And poses wend their sultry way

Down a path of physical abandonment;
These are the annals of our confinement--
Love-making in a sexual lust.

From off the pages of our Khama Sutra
Where the mat sways and energy's spent;
And emotions are jagged slivers
Of broken ice from a frigid environment;
These are the records of our endowment--
A cornucopia of libido dust.

From off the pages of our Khama Sutra,
Where the cave walls vibrate in concert
With the echoes of our calling;
Moans of delight and captured feelings meant
For the animus' of mates we haven't met--
Our sex is a kind of trust.

From off the pages of our Khama Sutra,
And we've composed a brand new book;
This tome is our momentary bible;
Its psalms the tenets of our mating;
Its depictions illustrations of our sating--
And climax is an emotional must.

And I like it when the snow falls;
It's white, it's pure, it's virginity,
Reminiscent of youth long before age.

Cosmic Fugue:

Now as I lay screaming in this
Fugue state that God has abandoned me
So irresolutely in;
Comprehension no longer eludes me
And I realize that I am dead.

"Impossible" thinks itself across the
Empty chasms of cranial thought;
A God can't die and evaporate;
A fishy carcass floating on the edge of sea.
Still I know, incontrovertibly,
That on that plane that I was in,
"I am dead."
   Gilgamesh travels the cosmos torn
So completely asunder; Its
Fabric is ripped and shredded.
And under this starry cloth of ether
Is a portrait he'd just as soon left
Unpainted. For in this fugue state
Was that place he so often dreamed of,
When in those fits of comas he'd relapse
Like a twitching fragile thing.
By that mountain with an Indian name,
Where he choked on the water of the river Jordan;
And when he'd gazed into its murky depths,
That certain someone who had exalted
In the sadism of his atoning.
And here she was reaching back
With all the tangibility
Of a spirit's unreal quality.
For in penance done and penance
More he'll always have to do.
Now she was in the waters without him.
He saw this hydrogenous simulacrum,
That liquid tableau of tortured grieving;
And knew that she was dead too.
No more would he be haunted in
That purgatory of intra-personal dreams;
In death he'd been awarded freedom,
From that earthy act of bereaving.
   I'm bent over and my knees are in pain.
How is it that from that state of fugue,
I am come to the Jordan where I imagined?
Two handfuls of dirt, and "Dust to Dust"
Ripples with my question across the water.
From beneath the water's edge I retrieve an urn;
A marble urn whose olive sides reflect the
Passing of the stream below; and I am hurting.

Innately I sense that these
Are the loamy remains of a wife and lover.
So in death she has come to set me free;
Tears come--profusely streaming
At the iniquity of it all.
I curse the one God
For his minute truths behind walls of
Concrete prisons represented as heavens.
And refuse to accept his judgement call,
Of death, dissonance, and mortality.
The ashes of my lover, which
I've taken from this Grecian urn,
Spurn the potency of fate and
Leave me no more sad or fallen.
I will steal some angel's wings,
And navigate back through these galaxies,
Back to the dearth of a good on earth,
And the search for a living wife and lover.
   Gilgamesh cries in a broken embrace,
With the urn, its green, its dust, and
Its reflected river's sheen; he's sifting
Through the ashes of what once was
A vibrant human being.
And love now will always be,
"A little less to me."

Arrogance:

   Oh how he laughed and purged the
Joy of capturing such a princess jewel as this;
A Magician come to rival God with purloinment
Of the best of Babylon,
And the idyll of a lover's single-minded mission.
He'd have his Gilgamesh wearing bracelets
In the tragic end.
But for him, Necromancer, there was

No tragedy baying hollowly across
The years he'd been contemplating the
Usurpation of the hegemony ruling heaven
That was so oppressing to him;
Necromancer would wear the crown
And Gilgamesh would play the jester
While God tapped out the beat on
The blade of the guillotine that
Was both instrument and executioner.
He suffered no shallowness in dreams;
He suffered no myopic disparities.
The addition of the breast of Babylon
And the acquisition of the knightly mission
Was the phalanx to lead the way;
Lofty ideals to use as tickets;
The price for acceptance into Eden.
Mephistopheles wearing the guise of saints,
And the halo of halogen purity.
His planning had no limits and
Carried with it the preciseness
Of a stonecutter's vision.
For from a carafe of distilled tinctures;
Admixtures steeped from the spirits
Of the souls held in captivity,
Magician would undermine the fabric being
Of heaven where those Idols sat so captivated;
Sadly drugged and bated.
He would offer them eternity
From the oat bag of a bitted horse in heat.
Better than the prescription living
Now extolled by God and his ministries.
Oh how he reveled in his potency
And bowed only to that one thing;
What was his latent quality,
What was his "Urge to Power."

Arousal:

A broken back, a splintered soul,
The remnants of a dream were what glued
The being that was left inside of her.
A lambent lichen blanketed the slimy
Walls of this grotto where Necromancer
Held sway over his rocky throne.
This green-y glow's what welcomed her
Upon the rough and wavy crests of her arousal;
It's what slapped her face and scarred
Her Retina like a razor swiped unwisely.
She vomited upon awakening, "Where am I?
What despot has taken me through
The ether and left me neither
Here nor there, wanting to be but anywhere?"
"It is I who is your captor,
I who holds in you such rapture,
I who as a raptor has become
Such a vicious but obsessive
Bird of Prey. You shall only
Leave here when I have been ensconced
As a regal lord of Eden.
And even then you will only wander
There as you did in your gardens at Babylon.
But in my heaven the butterflies will drip
With a caustic venom,
And dragonflies be your only solace;
Nooses and lariats will be the only flowers,
With the scents of summer nothing
But the noxious fumes of pepper gas.
But there you will tread the lilies
As my bride and lover;
For as I've watched you I've disrobed you,
And we've made love a thousand times,
All since you've lain unconscious;
I think I love you."

Living With a Ghost.

It's a park, it's a valley,
And the sun shines most illustriously.
They've just met; he his loneliness and
Her, her neediness. A common thread in
That co-dependent-ness. A quarry where
The stones always come out shattered,
No matter their preciousness.
But for now they do a lover's dance
Amongst the coagulation of fall leaves;
Those transient constituents of a changing season;
Where have all the good times gone,
And the fellows that used to beckon them?
God, she was so beautiful
And the corona of leafy diadems
Only wrapped a package of loveliness
That emitted a smile of innocence.
So they threw those leaves and played
And the games they wished were never ended
Seemed as if they'd go on,
In that immutable park, forever.
Sundown and an ashen burst of
Solstice glare waltzes across the
Naked branches of Oaks emitting
A warning foretelling the coming of November.
Will he ever someday remember
The name of the wife and lover who
Beckoned him from across the chasms
Of both mountains and latent dreams?
Or will he only clutch sporadically,
But faithfully, at her useless death
While elsewhere upon the planet
People toil with the trials of physical affairs?
How could he ever forget her;
How could he travel further
While breathing the dust that was her body,
And wearing the vomit of her dying?
It was only that he knew that somewhere
In that cosmic fugue where first he clutched
At human ashes; his soul had been entombed

Within the confines of her marble urn.
Never more to be set free, never more
To seek a holy union oft reserved
For only the un-lonely;
Her death wasn't the purge
Or the catharsis one expected it to be.
Sadly it buried itself to the hilt,
And the agony was a cat-o-nine tails
Flagellating him constantly.
    From the Freon of space was an angel
Watching diligently. And from her lid,
A bedroom lid which would cause a softness around
The edges of anyone's vision,
Issued a liquid trapezing itself across
Their lashes that were whispering--Sultry.
And she knew that she must be
The one that was to help him.
And he knew that he'd never forget her,
And that the echoes of his calling
Would always ricochet from off
The cavern of the finely polished urn.
Love would never find him;
Ideals would always haunt him;
And God would always, always taunt him.

Consummation:

    I'm shining and there's no Pyrrhic victory waiting for me;
My overcoming shall be absolute and the reason for our dying shall
Be written in the annals of some ancient text.
For, my love, such as you aren't, I'm back on earth and, My God
I am shining and it's no visual falsetto in sotto voce;
It is an argent beacon from a soul in super nova.
    The earth in meek rotation orbits across my vision
And I know that I am home; at long last home.
In the end God could not keep killed even a God like me.
I shall go to find my friend the Hunter who I know has not,

Like the others, abandoned me; I can sense his devotion to
Our special knightly-minded mission.
And I wonder, has he ever found her, that wife and mother
Who was taken suddenly on that night long ago?
One speaks of knives and daggers but never knows
The keenness of their edge until in agony it's
Brought across the throat of a screaming victim.
Such was the torture of my friend the Hunter
And the hollow chasm of a severed lover.
Can I ever find him again and if I do will he think
That I in desperation abandoned him?
      So with these thoughts tapdancing across neural membranes
And axion pathways steeped with a serotonin stain;
Gilgamesh entered the atmosphere and as he did
The friction of his entry cauterized the wound in his soul,
And melded his love that was two back into one.
The flame of coming home was the catharsis
That he needed to defeat the ignition
Coming from the conflagration of
Infinity spent among the volcanoes of purgatory;
The prospect of living was finally better.
      And there was Hunter and with him was another,
Walking towards the rising sun and the precipices
Of tumbling Ararat where Atlas had tripped and fallen.
And the impression of his landing was a chalk outline
Of a titan's slavery to eternity, with the Hunter and his
Momentary other marching through the powder that traced it.
And Gilgamesh for once was sincerely ecstatic, the joy
At the imminent meeting insufferable; he smiled.
The incandescence at his landing was blinding;
His effulgence both brilliant and demanding;
For at long last, as both Hunter and Valkyrie gazed in awe,
They all knew that Gilgamesh was indeed--A-shining.

The Coming of the Lord:

      The anger and the ire of the
Feelings of a jilted God are far worse
Than the juvenile grievings of that
Crossed up lover who so vindictively
Seeks their stilted revenge.
Such was the tension; the short circuit
Sparks emitting burst and pops in plangency,
Of God in his moldy chaise lounge,
By the stagnate, stench infested pool
Of rotting water lilies;
And served by the drug addicted angels
Whose folly was apparent by the
Swollen lids and senseless chuckles
Plastered on faces sans a joi de vivre.
Such was the mood in condescension
Of the tandem of God and heaven caused by
That fleeing, errant divinity
Who was almost better.
But God was so bitter;
In fact the angst was a blister,
Festering in his soul and carriage
Where only he could see it.
      And after the Atropine that
Was the alloy of earth and heaven;
The salve he had created, had
Failed to keep him imprisoned,
He decided to detection
Through his own enaction and
Would tread the earth himself,
Alone and unprotected.
Tossing aside the chalices of ambrosia
Which the cherubs chose to serve him
He trotted along the same path,
That Gilgamesh had taken so long ago;
He foot stepped where in Rebellion,
A cause and raison d'etre
Had flown with a choice to go.
He was in the pursuit of a
Thorn pinpricking the hubris of Apotheosis.

God was in a state of abdication,
Where no more nomenclature would apply.
On earth only the mission was
Ascendant and the jurisdiction of
Heaven held no authority.
And now as God stepped across
The threshold of Eden he dis-
Covered the daring of the "other."
And stood amazed at continuing,
Steeped with the impotency of a
Lord making an exit out of a kingdom.
      So God came to earth
With his own single-minded-mission;
To address his Gilgamesh;
To seek the reasons which
Embodied his laminated wish.
And as he came forth
One word kept its form;
Over and over again in a verbal libation,
An oral reproduction which
Would become the succubus of our lives;
--Impuissance.

Conversations:

      "Gilgamesh, I could have sworn that you
'd be dead, for when we were so discovered
I witnessed another form of abduction;
You were shanghaied ere the recollection
Of our cause of causes culminated in fruition."
      "A goddess coined Atropine created by
The ire of that God in heaven who so irately
Would have liked me better dead; perhaps
She is the one who executed the sentencing
Given without trial or even puppet jury.
In a cave I have been, cohort within a prison

With a leper who was a consolation
Recorded in annals left now unwritten.
She's gone, I did die, and that person of
Which I so often left a-dreaming,
Came and finally met me. She's dead also.
But the one God murdered me."
   "Gilgamesh, I am Valkyrie daughter of a friend,
Who felt your holy mission so misled,
And too feared that you'd be dead.
He sent me on this quest to free your soul
And now I fear that our goal so soon
Completed will leave me where I started;
Lost and dissolute; forlorn and desolate.
What is a vanquished Goddess to do, if
In the end I could not aid even you?"
   "Valkyrie, as a deity of degradation,
But a soul of lifted, lofty aspirations,
I can truly offer you something not found
In the distant, sepulchral, hallways of Sangri-la;
It's a cross not tattooed on the forehead;
It's a pieta without the body of the dead;
It's a trinity with one name left unsaid;
For in the rumblings of volcanoes and
In the throes of a turtle whose carapace
Is turned over on the ground,
It is the grand struggle of human beings.
Know we are icons cracked with imperfections.
Gods need desperately some sort of mission;
It is at the breast of doubt and need
That our souls should suckle
When famine strikes the fields of vanity."
   "Gilgamesh it is a wonder to see you thus;
So wise and humble but resolute none-the-less.
You are the basis for our saving
And the object of would-be graces
So that together we shall free our idyls.
Their cave is over there and
From here it's not far to an absolution;
So let us go and to the very end all
Our souls will be united with the thread
Which will weave the image in the
Tapestry creating the portrait of our lives.

If nothing else comes of it,
The trek in strident refrain
Screams-- "Worth It!"

Nadir:

       The three of them; the two Gods
And the valiant noble man; all
Strode resolutely on towards the
Culmination of that worldly mission.
Gilgamesh discovering the latent
Feeling wish that his needy, dreamy other
Somehow must now be there within
The confines of that temple in
Ebony thought and Demon cavern.
       And Hunter knew for certain that
The remnants of his wife and lover
Were there, hypnotized into comas and
That the refrain of her breathing was
All that signaled a sign of "life."
Yes she was alive and he would save her.
       Valkyrie sensed that only in
Victory; and not simply a Pyrrhic one,
Where the ages would scoff at the cost;
But one where that blanket of darkness
Which amassed such things as these:
Gods, fairies, and frail human beings,
Was completely come an outcast;
Only then would redemption be hers.
       Along a brook, a mature kind of
Rivulet; something some call babbling,
Padded only previously by the step of
Cats, bears, a deer, and a ferret;
Hyssop waved melodically with
The wind and the aroma-therapy
Of its scent spelling out--sustenance.

So the music, the scent, and the
Sustenance together walked forwards
In pale and solemn heraldry; their
Futures were told with the dangling
Of the willows across the trail and
In the sunlight that did not blister
Skins too long draped in darkness; it
Must have been some goodness filter
Erected by Magician to stave off what
Would be considered invaders. And
For some reason the trio did not
Notice the solar attenuation; for
While as bright the radiance appeared
Tenebrous to the point of sunless.
And a fierce melancholy overtook them.
Sadness was now their reason, and
Each footstep a hollow clank
Against the bars of something coined,
--Depression.
They were getting closer.

Alba:

The syllables of a rhyme echo from out
A tower constructed with the intent of watching;
Observing a pacing sentry now uncaging
The prosody of the lines within him;
And the sun's first burst of brightness
Evokes the phrases ending in "Alba."

Oh the melodic harmony as steep-y night
Offers self for the coming of dawn and day.
She's subservient, she isn't unwilling.
And the poesy of the watchman's refrain lets
Them while twilight recedes in fluctuation;
Their moans of delight crooning "Alba."

So in metrical union dawn is dominant

And the act of day and night compelling;
While still wailing that guardsman seems
The whole world to be telling and
Is it indeed a sentry's warning of
Things maybe a-coming with his "Alba?"

Now somewhere in the land of Gilead
Two lovers un-wrestle and in glimpsing
First minute hinting of an end of play;
They mourn lovers' unrestrained servility;
Though they never think of separation,
The ritual cessation is heralded by "Alba."

But it is a union possible to continue
Given the communion of holy vows,
So that if love is given validation,
Then the midnight susurration can be,
A midday alteration model of validity;
And that warning sentry a 24 hour "Alba."

Terminations:

    Now on approach to Devil's encampment,
The trio and a fourth: Hope,
Clawed away at the nearing feeling of
Once impending; sad and wilting, doom.
They were afraid.
They'd heard the sentry's warning wail;
That sense of yearning and wished,
That the two Gods were whole,
And Hunter one of them.
But still they trod on.
    Broken paths and shattered rocks
Were what greeted them at this
Their journey's impending plot.

Desperation clouded their quietness,
And every tripped up rock was a
Pounding on Hell's backdoor.
Then through the filtered brightness,
They heard a scurrying of sundry feet;
They heard the clip-clop of
Cloven hooves and impish pleats.
They heard a chuckling anticipation
Carried upon the pants of thousands,
Of green-winged demons.
And as they crested the last
Rock encapsulated trail-head,
Columns of these henchmen greeted
Them as if they were already dead.
No longer intrepid steps
Ricocheted across the canyon,
And they heard in it,
The drumming of their graves.
Between the columns of lined up
Devils was a trail dissecting
The bowels of the fortress;
Ending in a gravity swell; where
They knew their presence was
Not so very unexpected.
      Slavering mouths and dripping
Suppurating eyes lavished greed
And avarice upon them.
Now in unison every creature
Every bent and broken Dybbuk raised his
Scarred and scratched up arm.
And with awareness pointed;
Straight to the portal of hell,
Right to that light less well;
And courage and resolve,
Like an unplumed bird, fell.
They were scared.
Then Gilgamesh in brief remembrance
Of his deceased lover, whom
He'd never really met;
Straightened up his wilting back,
Raised his head and said
That, "We've come so far,

To give ourselves a reason;
We'll not succumb to doubtful thinking,
At the threshold of our freeing,
More than just our would-be lovers.
We have a mission to uphold;
We have our--dignity,
And we have our--Will to live."
    So with this said they all
Joined hands in standing side by side;
In commemoration of human equality;
They quelled the numbing of
The buzzing in their bowels.
They strode together into Gehenna,
To face a Beelzebub who
Had come into some power.
If all else was to fail,
Then at least on the verge of
Life in hell, their fear,
They had finally,
Come to Conquer.

Ignominy:

    As God stepped on earth,
He realized in quick depth
Of minute understanding,
That he had indeed never
"Been here before!"
So he cried to himself and
Mumbled, "I'm so afraid and
So very, very all alone."
That Gilgamesh strode here
Before him was all that
Kept the one God going.
    At first landing he
Stumbled into a town where
In his soiled robes and

Unkempt manner people thought him
Another vagrant not quite
Regal enough for charity,
Or uncompassionate pity.
God took to nightly wandering;
Wondering where he'd find
That Gilgamesh; never realizing,
That in the end he'd
Already murdered him.
      One night as God
Lay below a tavern door
Where the proximity of
Vivacious people seemed,
As a touch of Alcohol,
To comfort him;
Even though he was not
One of them;
Two drunkards poured the
Remnants of their beer on him.
So with this baptism of
Tainted water God felt
The misery imbued by the father,
Upon the shoulders of the son.
With the shards of broken
Bottles laying in the gutter,
God picked a tunnel to lie in
And methodically cut his wrists.
Now with the solitude of death
Stentorian in its breath upon
His sometime supine back,
God began to shudder. And
Asked himself, "Why, oh why,
Could this be happening to me?"
The rich, red, ichor poured
In uncanny circles
Around the body of the dieing.
      Then a cry, a shout, a
Loudly vociferous extirpation
Of unholy doubt emitted
Itself from the ceiling
Of the starry night.
God in misery had been found;

Now two-fanged bats,
Brothers of the others,
Appeared to steal this
Moribund soul away.
What a sacred treasure,
What a papal pleasure;
Would that Magician take in
Discovering that on earth,
As it does not in heaven,
The blood of God thickens,
And like the agony of humans,
It congeals and hearkens,
To an age of evolution
And primordial hunger.

Culminations:

Three cowls and horses parked,
Three riders in the dark.
They stood by Necromancer
As seconds and lieutenants.
It was the inquisition
Of innocence or burden of proof.
They were grimly waiting,
For what now is known.
Off in the corner were
The meek and comatose induced
Figures in submission
Of two ladies held in lieu.
A tacit duo in reverence
To something called beauty.
And on a dais upon a throne,
A marble, golden-gilded
Seat built of stone sat
Sepulchral majesty;
That travesty of magicians

Who tainted holy missions,
With his urge to power.
And the chamber was itself
Both black and light
Featuring chiaroscuro,
Where bats in recesses
Grinned with boasting.
And a flame was burning
Within the center of
Some Psychic, Satan stones.
Above those green-hued
Flames, wherefrom issued
No smoky emanations,
Was suspended in sad
Astuteness to a Zeit-Geist,
God was held by the leather
Of a whip to an upright Ankh.
And the blood of his wounds
Into conflagration still was dripping,
Made senses seem somewhat
Close to lacking, by
Mere act of inhaling
The incense of this un-
Real, imaginary desecration.
All constituents of this
Pre-meditated confrontation,
Waited in anticipation;
For that Gilgamesh, and
Alter-egos Hunter and Valkyrie.
Whose footstep reverberations
Beat out but one
Word in a Morse-code:
Cul-mi-na-tion.

The Arrival:

It was that promised land
Where at the end of life a
Compensation would be delivered

For all the years of strife,
Pain and human suffering;
That holy grail of godhood,
Known as Gilgamesh, had
Come to take possession.
And he wondered if he was
What some call living; or simply
A pretender to the throne
Of the innate stage of dieing.
This as he waltzed into the
Chamber of the flying, smokeless,
Suspended, green-y embers where
All the demons gathered round;
Magician sat mute with sound;
And bats in recesses hung down;
Where twin lovers lay in state,
Horsemen stood in wait, and God;
God was hanging from an Ankh,
By the leather of a whip, and
Was not what Gilgamesh had remembered.
Open wounds seeped a mucous,
From wrists a-gaping;
And Gilgamesh in a fit
Of a kind of prescience,
Sensed that the one God was no longer
Mad or angry at.
When all the thespians
In this pent up play of penitence;
Actors in their final dramatic act;
Were accounted for; present,
There was a communal
Feeling of frenetic relief.
And the sighs were let in unison,
With a common beat;
Almost were all these fancy
Players of the field resting,
--Asleep.

The Swarm:

"Antipathy seems to be the
Antagonism of our little fete;
With your loves no longer enough.
I have both your missions
Asleep in hypnotic knots.
So quoth the Magician who
Is the nemesis of your calling;
The impasse to swollen empathy.
I'll snap my fingers and demonstrate
The futility of your coming; with
The awakening of your birds I'll be
The object of indiscreet idolatry.
For they no more love you!"
    With that their eyes began
To flitter and flutter; like
Monarchs on Birches landing;
These two brides aroused;
Sitting now they gazed around.
    "So Magician you've captured
What would be lovers, and
Eviscerated the bowels of the one God.
You've raped maybe companions, and
Made them drink the blood of God.
But our hope is not so weak,
As ice in one hundred degrees of heat.
Our faith in overcoming is not
A pillaged repository of Nikes;
Beheaded and buried beneath
The skeletal remains of bones.
We shall persevere."
    With that commanding oration
In the face of a dominating Magician,
Gilgamesh empowered the Hunter,
Causing him to speak; thus:
    "I may be mere mortal; an
Imperfect being who embodies no
Salient or potent powers of freeing.
But I am undefeatable and will
Kiss the hand of my wife who's

The mother of my children now waiting
For the return of our mating."
      And Valkyrie felt the urge,
To stipulate a puissant admonishment
To the arrogance of Necromancer,
And his too confident tone;
He who held the refrain
Of an orchestra
In the sweaty palm of his hand.
      "I am immortal, a Goddess,
Who has done battle with the
Forces of the three behind you.
No I did not, could not,
Conquer those dread foes, but
Have returned to free
The enslaved souls of those
Held in your contemptuous court.
I am humility personified,
I am hubris dignified."
      The three horsemen began to
Spin with Magician's magic then.
They in revolution did make,
A hoary blackness gravitate
Across the chasm to the fire;
Which then enveloped the
Purity of visitors to the chamber;
It ensconced the decent fibers
Of the strangers to this cave;
Where evilness willed to reign.
And Hunter, Valkyrie, and that
Gilgamesh imploded; three
Deep sub-sea mariners
Crushed by the ocean gravities.
      "Noooooo," Came in one sudden
Anthropomorphic wail of human
Refusal to accept indignity.
Mycenaean Queen, that princess
Had felt the fait-accompli
In the vapors of God's blood;
Had felt the presence of the dreamy,
Sultry lover who of she'd
Been waiting for.

And now grew angry at
The prospect of--Mate-less.
Screamed, "Un-acceptable!"
She screamed, "Un-repressible!"
She screamed in essence,
To fight for the loss of love.
"Never will I accept
The turmoil of life in a weedy garden
As a Queen to an inept farmer.
Gilgamesh you must now contain,
The stealing of your own willful elan;
You must reject this procuring,
Before he invades your bi-polar,
And manic, self-effacing idolatry.
For I am she and you are he,
And together we've bided these
Years of anticipation to seek
Out the other within us;
And I do love you."
      Oh the strength that
Can be deducted from those
Simple mono-syllabic mots
Of feeling and wanting.
The needing was apparent,
And Gilgamesh uprose with the others;
To face the reprisal of a
Thaumaturgy so dispensed
Without the dust of power.
And so came awake that
Classic wife and mother to
Rejuvenate the face of Hunter.
      "My husband, I need you!
I don't even know what happened,
Just that I've been captured;
And oh, how are the children?"
      "My wife that was first a lover,
Who became a mother in the beauty
Of the birth of children; I'm
Elated at last in finding
Wherein this earth you'd
Been stolen and taken.
And I will free you from

This cave of oppression, to
Reunite us with our children.
And occurrences such as these
Can be summed up by the one
Word known as-- 'never.'"
        And from the holy pendulum,
Above the green-y pyre, where
Embers twirled and spun so higher;
Came a whisper, and a murmur,
As of life's emanations exuding
Its last impression of vitality
Upon the psyche of those left living.
God was speaking:
        "Gilgamesh, I am so sorry;
Why could I not know that
In heaven Gods need lovers too.
That what is a scarce commodity,
Is just a chance necessity.
That undying adoration to another
Single soul of souls,
Was greater than the sum of whole;
Eden, heaven and even pristine
Gilead, all meant nothing,
When in suspension love was
Measured by degrees of idolatry; and
Prostate and genuflecting devotion
To me. That I was not the end
Of a struggle; just the druggy
Termination to footsteps march for eternity.
That before subservience to me
One must be in equality with
That mate and loving paramour.
Adam and Eve were not the sinners;
Just the novices in the art of loving;
And I was jealous at their pleasure,
So sent the serpent and the savior.
The fruit of life should
Have been free; not taxed
With sin and guilt, and yes,
Even the weight of conscience.
That, Gilgamesh, is my confession,
And you become my confessor;

Please forgive me,
For I as a wretch am a sinner."
      And so the one God on
Earth went away unconscious;
Paler from the act of bleeding.
And Necromancer stood snapping
With the sound of
One hand clapping;
Bringing an end to this tearful reunion
Of joyful recognitions.
      "How touching; how adorable,
Is all this connecting;
God accedes and Gilgamesh forgives;
Missions seek fruitions,
And Valkyries sense a victory.
Horsemen begin to wonder,
And bats in recesses shiver and ponder;
Demons doubt and I grow angry;
While you all are truly
Still at the whim of my mercy."
      So chanting "Ishtar, Hecate," and something
More cutting, Magician invokes the moon.
All pure souls slam back against
The crystal granite of the walls.
And all the allies swoon.
Gilgamesh is launched into the fire,
Bringing an eerie glow to the room.
He hollers in agony,
Hollow at thoughts of deprecation,
Loss, and suffering.
He can't breathe.
It is then they know
The power of this Mephistopheles;
That here in grotto God's a beggar,
And Valkyrie had given her
Immortality passionately away.
Gilgamesh had denounced the
Presence of divinity within his
Needful being; impotence around
All their fingers formed a ring.
Wife and mother, princess and lover,
Both reeled back in attitudes

Of willingness to promiscuity.
Revealing breasts to thaumaturgy.
All was at an end; and
Love would not conquer.
The two women would be pregnant,
With the children of the raper,
Making of them whores.
And all the others would be eunuchs,
At the double birth.
"The end" seemed to echo
In migration across the cavern.
Necromancer, his hooded eyes,
His traipsing hair in falling locks,
Began to dance and holler,
Forming a trance nearer to the pyre;
It was over!
      Stentorian in magnitude came a wave
From the Dome of the Rock;
A guttural vibration of
Monumental stock. It quickly
Built to unbearable proportions,
To culminate in the explosion
Of imprisoning rocks.
Shards of gneiss missil-ed only
Into the beings of the demons,
And beheaded the fearful dybbuks.
Horsemen's cowls were baked;
With skulls devoid of
Cover they were alchemically
Spent and slaked; harmless
Now, just bones; no gristle;
They lay on the earth simply shaking.
Necromancer knocked back by the
Shock of unforeseen attack;
Wanted only to see the source
That had made him so quickly lax.
And the first little tendril
Of red-rimmed fear or doubt,
Fought its way to the surface.
Straight from over the flames
Beyond the Dome of the Rock,
Came approaching a candle

So illuminatingly bright that
It was thought
A miniature sun intact.
It landed upon the floor of the cave,
And the glow rescinded to become
The embodiment of girl in corona;
A mistress to cosmic fallacies.
God and Gilgamesh managed together,
To utter aloud her argent identity:
"Atropine, the alloy of earth and heaven!"
She had come from the hills and
Dales of a typhoid earth originally
To imprison and seek a vengeance;
But with the abscondment of the
One God she'd felt the
Temporal imbalance of a weight,
With no mass-y balance, come
To take over the tandem of earth and heaven.
She'd felt for Gilgamesh a
Strangely lucid compassion,
Though she'd imprisoned,
And went to free him only to
Discover his soul deceased,
Running rampant in the cosmos.
Somehow she knew God and Gilgamesh
Would be found together.
So she'd followed the portents
In the trails of useless power;
Just to arrive in the nick of time;
Just now at the scene of the
Ethereal, unreal crime.
  "Necromancer, it is you who
Will be so deceased; ended now before
Your beginning has begun. You are history."
  "What makes you so certain; you who are
Merely a lackey to the one God who hangs
Now, a Roman tribute to subjects of
A central throne? What causes you to
Think that you can defeat the mastery of
A darker knight whose armor is replete
With amulets imbued with carnal might?
I who has slept with the lunar maiden;

Changing the orbit of a moon is not
Something you could dream of doing."
   "Your arrogance is disgusting
For it will make your falling seem
All the more plummeting and your
Passing so much more rewarding. For
When God saved me from the burning
Stone where volcanic vultures sacrificed;
Thus making me more than the sum of one;
He inadvertently created the chasuble
Of all that was good in heaven; and
Beautiful on the face of the earth. I
Am the nectar of the Rhodora fermented
Into plenary, steep-y, and viscous concoctions.
To combat the atavism of ones as you.
I am all that is pure; all
That the one God thought he was;
Spelled by the one word of--trust.
He unwittingly created a Queen,
For the first flank of God.
And now you must deal with everything:
Usurpation, torture, and the stomping
Of neo-knightly missions."
   With that Necromancer hurled a
Coruscating laser at her heart;
Never knowing that it would merely
Boomerang merely back,
Hitting him in the chest; he
Was still in a state of shock.
Atropine in response unsheathed a bolt
Of lightening held incandescent;
Launching it at burning target.
The nuclear radiance of impact brought
An end to this coup d'etat;
Of Magician's collecting prey.
He vaporized like the mist of
Morning ere a sunny day. He
Was now just a memory burned
Onto the boulders right below.
And Atropine flung her arms
Making everyone free to go
From the bowels of nefarious palace,

Where destiny had painted upon a surreal
Tapestry to display the event of
Its holy entry. And they all crawled
From the pressure of that chamber.
With Atropine carrying God and her summons.
Gilgamesh escorting his new-found lover;
Hunter his heart of hearts;
Valkyrie supporting her dignity
Across shoulders crying for Asgaard.
No one yet could speak or make
Speech seem a priority. Oration
Was a momentary impossibility,
Until clear of the tomb where
Innocence indeed was lost.
They just kept trod-ding until
That nighttime fell across the mountain
Side of the land of the East.
There by the river Nile they en-
Camped away from the revelry of
Humans and godly play; the
Quiet was a blanket of reflection
With which they held near to the
Other to whom each was dear;
They slept the sleep of the dead.
Thought in panic no more in head.
  And in the morning came time
For all to part in separate ways;
Hunter with wife and mother said farewell,
To the others but the Hunter stayed a
Touch longer; held back to hug that Gilgamesh
Whom had been confidante and companion.
  "Well Hunter you are off, back
To the boundaries of a normal life;
Without you my mission would have
Been deemed incomplete for not
Just a lover did I make but
Found a friendship that salves charred
Remains of a cathartic soul."
  "Gilgamesh, you've shown me
That Gods are not so aloof-ish, so
Much merely monolith idols in temples,
Who breathe only incense, and pass

The blood and ambrosia of divinity;
While one hand takes a tithing and
The other metes out a justice. You,
I must admit, are better off human;
And I'm glad to call you a friend.
   Valkyrie, you too have become
Much more than that idolatry; now
Become a hidden memory treasure; a
Trove or chalice from which drink
Was both salubrious and strong; potent.
Our journey together though arduous and long,
Was the challenge of my life, and
I, for one, will never forget you!"
   "Hunter, when back in Asgaard
Where revelry is a kind of home, and
I'm drinking with my brethren
To a holier kind of union;
My mind will be on you; and
We shall be drinking together again
As once we did so far away from Dome."
   With their tearful farewells said;
Hunter and his wife departed; fuller,
Though sadder for some reason; perhaps
For the knowing that Gods could be
More human than they ever wished to see.
   "Gilgamesh, Atropine and I are in
Process of leaving; back to refurbish an
Eden left untenable by avarice and exit
Of fleeing Gods; we shall make it better.
I leave you to your own devices; to
Live with and as whom you desire;
You have my devoutly given blessing;
And wish you well in your quest for loving.
Further I grant you full freedom to
Cherish a life of Gilead's godhood
Or exalt in this world of men; it's
Your choice, it's your decision, and
I give it freely, I give it
Willingly with no penance due for
Penance you've already done."
   "One God, I thank you for my freedom,
For in the offering you've joined the

World of humans and their loving; I
Therefore choose an innate destiny of
My deciding and my very own. It's
Truly all I ever really wanted,
And all I ever sought; so
I opt to be here with her,
For no godhood could be all
That exists in the mind of dreams,
Without the thought of only she.
Now that I've found her I'll
Never be but three steps beside
Her, and closer still as
Until we're completely re-united.
But one God there is one request
That I feel must be granted and
I think you know my innermost wish;
Both our atonements are come dependant
On accomplishment of said wish;
And I'd like to do it."
  "Yes you're right my Gilgamesh,
To support this and I condone it,
As your last act of godly mien,
I empower you with this final request;
You have my permission.
Make this desire a reality, and
We'll both feel the state of--rested."
  With that the one God
And his Atropine went off to
Rehabilitate a dependant disordered heaven.
Cherubs required straightening, and
Seraphim some questioning; then
The oil from the water separating, and
Placement in vials for consecration of souls.
Beauty would now be enjoyed by couples,
Instead of the hypnosis of ones; that
Balm in Gilead would never again
Be absent, or left a-wanting.

The Ending:

They rode in on the eve of festival
When cherry blossoms were the
Best of all the flowers celebrated,
For the coming weeks of holidays.
That Princess had returned was
Immediately apparent for the pall
That previously had been so obvious,
Dissipated like sunshine at dusk;
People stopped in steps held dear,
They whispered in voices, "It's her,"
And wondered aloud about the stranger
Whose regal carriage emitted--noble.
But all knew that princess returned
Bearing a beauty unfathomable,
Accompanied by man unreadable.
And they were happy for the coming
Of the best of Babylon was lovely.
She strode with him to the gates
Of the palace previously called home.
The guards the gates they opened with awe,
At the healing of kingdom torn
Once, and thought ever, asunder.
Straight to the garden paths where
She used to dream of sultry lover;
Straight to the trodden chambers where
She'd dreamt of a midnight paramour.
Where once memories were so lonely,
And feelings dissolute and stony,
At thought of never discovering,
What she knew was so alluring;
Had haunted her very soul.
And to stand so here in hallways
Where his dreamy lover had waited,
So long held to elusive fidelity.
Where no reward seemed forthcoming;
Gilgamesh was at last validated.
As if the sense of smell he'd needed,
Finally bore aroma of violets, or
Odor of country morning hamlets;

His spirit screamed--satiated.
        Out in the garden by the Azaleas,
And a leafy, brachiated Acacia;
These two lovers finally met, for
They had not touched; not yet.
For the tension of story complete,
Was a form of barrier causing
Togetherness to seem indiscreet.
So they'd waited till each was sure,
That amorousness was okay;
That love, devotion, and fidelity,
Weren't catchwords of an oblique day.
With fingers upright and touching,
Face to face, eye to eye, each
Breathing the others breath, they
Stared as if all the world were
Witness to a new found wonder;
And love; they knew that love,
Was finally, finally theirs.
He his mission, his holy quest;
Her, her waiting, her faithfulness;
The twain at last did kiss;
And tears of togetherness sprinkled
The tufted grass whereupon a
Musical rustling could be heard.
Little murmurs and wispy shouts,
That make sense only in temples,
And castles and far off lands,
Where living isn't so mechanical;
And adoration not simply fiscal.
They were something that tinkles,
When glass bells are jingled;
For if you'll sit by a brook whose
Banks in front of it stumbles,
When quietly the water, the Robins,
The crickets who in cloister sit,
Are all the conversation to be pondered,
You'll hear those whispered rumors
Of proud Princess and that
Knightly missioned Gilgamesh.
You'll hear the three words softly delivered;
Not effete, nor hackneyed, but

As they were always supposed to be;
The ones they told each other,
Who was to each a savior:
Darling, darling; truly,
"I love you!"

Epilogue

It's a bar, a smoky den; and a dancer
Undulates off in the distance. But it's
Not this pure bred pony who oscillates,
Who was once a slut in this menagerie.
She's free from that sad calling now; and
Simply stopped in for a drink or two,
To have with her husband of only a
Few days; though the engagement was
Years of lonely hours spent in that
Solitude of gangrenous lepers.
Flesh once rotten was healed--better;
Veil once held in tatters together,
Now whole and superior; for too,
Her psyche reeked of adhesiveness.
And these two were happy; for the loss
They once had suffered was each other.
And the love they once felt was no
Longer something each had to share,
With an illicitly tipping other.
His handsomeness was a sight she
Had before only remembered; but now
Recognized in a stark, chemical timbre.
She breathed a gasp of thoughtfulness,
To the friend or God who'd done this.
He asked why happy she was crying?
And the smile of her reply was the answer.
She only nodded and said t'was time to go.
Said they had some candles to light,
In a solemn worship to the one God,
Who now she'd come to a reverence; in

A perfect harmony of faith in adoration;
She came to the disenchanted temple,
To kneel before a dusty, dirty altar.
Deserted apses and hollow halls greeted
Her dissonant chant of holy prayer.
For this God had once lost favor, and
With such descent his popularity;
So his priests tired and defected.
But she preferred it this way; more
Loving and more intimate were
Her alluring chants and special sayings.
"I can't be a-coming anymore, we're moving,
And there aren't any old temples left where
We're going in that land of painted pharaohs;
Where once your following was so able.
But I just wanted to tell you what in
Person I had no opportunity to utter,
And that is my heartfelt thank-you.
You to me are the only God and
Indeed I know I'll always love you!"
    A blow, a puff, this paragon of girl
Exhales across the candle; it's dim.
She rises, turns and wafts towards
The hallway and its exit doors.
Her husband there awaits and he grasps
Her hand in devotions sake to guide her
From out the maze of the overgrown path,
And the weedy, untended frolicking garden.
Now beneath a full moon she gazes back
Seemingly lost in a haze of memories;
She smiles a tear and loves that one
God who had thought to save her.

    With a shudder and a tremble-throb,
It's that sweet-and-sour happyish;
    With a mutter and a treble-sob,
"I bid thee adieu, Gilgamesh."

About the Work

This dramatic poem is dedicated to the memory of Connie Ann Bond who died incognito and alone—and, worse yet, knew it.

The Tarantella—A Sequel

Akhenaten

Solar disc and arid days but
With a verdant wisp mascaraed
On the edges of the symbol of life.
It's an ankh, it's a flowing coronary
In rhythm leaping little cataracts.
Here we sit peasants begging for cause
Where lovers are sisters and sodomy
A reason for life. Nefertiti mas-
Sages herself and pleases me with
Lips meant for simple teasing; I
Can sense the tingling of teeth
In a stranger kind of motion; an
Ascending-descending asp-y kind of
Commotion whose vacillations are
Consummation on a sunny morning.
       The satisfaction with vassal women
Waving wispy fronds whose breath is
Sensual as they breathe across the
Oil-lotion whose chilly fibers
Offer erotic precipice on brink of
Chasm; I think of second portal where
Her fingers begin to wander and ponder
Upon the brink of hers too; it's a
More succinct form of passion.
Deeper--my digits tear asunder the
Forbidden act supplied by nature.
Now--a bucking maelstrom; a
Cavorting sandstorm clouds a vision
That had been laser perfect. We
Are one who were-two and it's time
To mount the threshold of purity,
Where my soul does as it should.
And my shoulders arch and she swallows;

Peristalsis consumes the sundry liquid;
She exudes some of her own.
My fingers protrude and a visceral
Moan concludes in an almost groan;
Its profundity is a teary wail wanting more.
Exploring my fingers venture further
Nefertiti's solemnly willing tunnel:
God Aten, I'm so sure that I love her!
      That done we direct the slaves
To denude themselves of robes and
Garments and sultry things in the
Morning heat. And Nefertiti takes
Them any way while a Pharaoh resides
Within them. Satin throbs and
Lotus leaf insertions mix with the
Musk of carnal pheromones creating;
Just-insisting a sort of mating;
Cunning in their length of sating;
Lips on lips breath abating; I can't
Contain the organ gasping; as if
In brief seconds eons passing capt-
Uring lapping waves of vulnerability.
In mutual heap I finally taste
The oozing of un-sutured lust and
Woman's most swollen kind of need.
--I want wine, I want security, I want
The approval of the God Aten:
Into the apse at the base of heaven,
I enter-seemingly thrusted in.

Intermezzo

    The temples have crumbled and
I'm all that's left; the sordid priests
    Ran some time ago leaving me;
A sacrifice on the altar of love.
    Was I taped? Was I chained to
That dimpled granite whose stone
    Was reminiscent of sexless shores?

I don't know but experiencing such
    Strange emotions emoted longing
And shock, both, at being tied
    And abandoned; what is called alone.
Now I just want to come back home.
    I want love and friendship;
Maybe even some sensual com-
    Panionship; You know; some
Of that human loving where
    The touch is the stare is the tingle
In our soul; that animal throne.
    So I'm back from the desolate
Saharas and bleakly weathered
    Lapses of mental solitude. I'm back--
And thought I'd say hello to you.

Nefertiti

"Ad Ashti Per Sempoza En Senchal"
Cried Nefertiti to her self; over again
While lying alone in the tresses of the
Arboretum lining the littoral of the Nile
Along the Portico of Palatial doors.
"Ad Ashti Per Sempoza En Senchal"
Cried Nefertiti to herself; out loud
While wading knee-deep through water
Which had come from Lake Victoria.
In a pas-de-deux, her-self and she,
She trembles over pebbles and yearns
Tangibly for the other spiritual coast
Where Pharaohs, Queens and Men
Are untinctured divinity.
"Ad Ashti Per Sempoza En Senchal"
Cried Nefertiti to herself; whispering
While the diaphony of her gown melded
With the solace of her skin and left the
Lissomness of figure and breasts and limbs
Taut with a yen for need and questioning.
She drops the holy Sarong sensing the

Concrete breccia beneath spirit-like feet;
She wonders what it's like to please Aten;
If he'd smile at the human inspirations;
Nascent aspirations tongued in a language
Unheard of and then--would he love her too?
"Ad Ashti Per Sempoza En Senchal"
Cried Nefertiti to herself; in a tenor
Through the reeds and the cedar trees;
Where Orioles and Bumble bees wrought
Arias and harmonies composed as serenades,
Sung in melodic threnodies. Such
Herbarium sensory so stimulated the
Atmosphere, whose ozone heated electrically,
Nefertiti thought she'd clutched Aten.
But Alas, the solar disc lay up in Heaven,
And she lay on earth convulsing, and
Nothing changed but perspective, and
Her strength now waned and ebbed.
"Oh God in Heaven--please take me now."

The Dream

Incarnadine and verdigris and ver-
Million; these are the colors of
My life somehow: picture tubes:
I imagine--
In my arms the motion twists the
Nature around and around in circular
Devolutions of pining; of moving; of
Tempest tossed paeans of yearning.
I imagine--
The girl in my arms is you and
All the words once written: of bats,
And Penserosos in chairs, and stars and
Stares, were still etched somewhere
Other than on a granite cenotaph
Where your image looks like Mary
Praying, and grass is always
Delicately manicured and holes are
Dug neatly squared; no round or

Softly sculptured figures there.
I imagine--
There is a song mellowing and
We gently swaying, absolution to
Absolution emoting a common breath:
Tiny little cups of lips on eyelids;
And I aid you getting dressed like
Symbiotes in musky jungles mesmer--
Ized; languor in new-found ellipses;
Beginnings with no endings.
I imagine--
Androids shattering stained-glass
Panes of icons demanding adoration.
Kristal nacht takes on a whole new
Meaning; has no origin on earth;
Except in eruptions of volcanoes;
Block-fault quakes with their
Epicenters in starry spheres.
Cataclysm becomes a baptism with
Anubis to hold one's hand; the Jackal
Scavenges and I count the vultures.
Akhenaten shall go to heaven--
I imagine.

Thumbelina

Thumbelina was raped yesterday.
Brutal: now the composition of molecules
Is arranged in images like enantiomers
Where components differ by atoms of
One. What could be said or done to
Ease the pain of graphic violation. I
Always thought that heaven would
Be a safer place than ions in hell.
      She screamed; she ran; she cried;
The rending of her gowns cried, "No!"
Violation was the intimation of her soul.
They took her--more than one: no inter--
Diction could make the sublimation
Acceptable; Thumbelina was forced into

Submission in legions of happy beings
Sipping wine on the eternal median of Astral
Equinox. But She deserved it you say? The
Dirt; the filth; the face with rivulets of tears.
"She didn't ask for this."
Inknaten didn't mean to do it.
Was it the double helix that took him up to
Heaven; the lettered stairway held--responsible?
                      Chrysalis fractured in Edenic heat;
                      The crush of flesh by flesh and
                      Visceral beat timed in groans of
                      Agony. Thumbelina's wings were
                      Ripped right off her back and the
                      Sound of gown, throat and legs,
                      Were whispers wafting in the air.
                      No cerebration of help impressed
                      Itself upon the angel thoughts
                      Who just left her in despair: Why?
                      Years of purity deep inside shredded
                      By angelic complicity—What's a girl
                      Supposed to do--but submit and live.
                      Ah, the breadth of this fairy-tale,
                      Where the thrust is the wish is the
                      Whisper of stealth in Armageddon.
                      Inknaten lost his senses.
Yes, Thumbelina was raped yesterday and
God and Heaven and Christ are held
Accountable for the presence of the monotheist.
But it's said he had a right to take her:
He was a Pharaoh come to heaven;
She was a woman unleavened--
But why that Thumbelina?
Crumbling--a smile.

Byzantium

Temples with golden figures blowing
Horns entrancing millions: walls of granite
All around and deciphered chicanery a

Rococo on the cornice of the mosque.
Hirundine--a bird titters on the brink
Staring at last at the sculpture embracing
Money with his back disdaining temple.
Hills standing sentinel to indoctrination
And a salt sea foaming in the distance;
But no ships traffic there, the Bosporus
Sits a fifteen mile Via Apia where Belial
Reigns at its head--confluence of devout
Religion and smiling hyenas selling
Shares in the bazaar of agora, square and
Marketplace: this is the religion of the dead.
Little creeks and maple trees adorn the
Fallacy of the pristine that used to be--
Now Byzantium rests sophisticated instead.
Apostles jingle francs in bordellos whose
Sangria-laden lips of whores dance in
Species of Hagia Sophias every Sabbath:
Albescence in symbols of some purity.
Inknaten knew this was the place to find
The Teutonic stairs to heaven: authority.
Across the Mediterranean on reed ships
With Nefertiti and homunculus to
Chronicle the holy passage: Scribe.
There in ordered streets of multi-
Cultural minions, who Scribe will put
On papyri sheets, this trio will journey
To demesne of Heaven and tip the goblets
With God and Christ and holy men;
Will frolic with amorous bent around
Frustrated and pent, servant seraphim.
Theirs is an endeavor in print.
Tapped delicately
In little figures of hieroglyphs.

Dismantling of Stonehenge

A swollen land; turf spelled tramontane;
Where we once were met.
You know, the Townhouse, East Gate,
Iron Horse at the top of the hill?
      But that was then and time had her
Sultry, wanton and errant predator way.
I was party to an act which I've come
To fear has had a part in the play which
Has portrayed the separation of Stonehenge;
Whose once articulate lines graced blank paper
With such images few artists had talent to tell.
You know: Cities, houses in Batik and
Portraits held icons of still-life.
Yes Stonehenge could do more than that:
Those crafted blocks were an orchestra
Held by seraphim when the wind came;
Notes: A-minor, C-major, keeping half-time
With strings first strung by Pythagoras,
Who knew the tonal qualities would outlast
Even the Grecian tincture of his name.
But you, too, Stonehenge whose monument
Is now silent held muffled; mercenary;
Buffeted of all wind—doesn't your
Muse let you sing anymore or strum
In tribute to a holier kind of union?
Once even the pen of Stonehenge wrought
Such calligraphy of recondite thought;
Are there no more tales left in the ink
Etched upon the facets of obelisk? Or
Has the sandstorm of living eroded them to
Rounded lumps of illegibility?
Has Stonehenge been so disassembled
That he discounts all the worthwhile
Thoughts proffered as ideals by a cabal
That was more than a meeting of youth?
We weren't but young but otherworldly then
When those things of what we spoke
Were truly all that was; and now you speak
Of aging, responsibility and matrimony still.

Rather speak of idylls better regained again
Than sunk and scuttled like wrecks at sea.
   I shudder to think that though
I didn't remove the first few stones,
I helped to change the composition of
The binding cement that was a mortar;
The bones in the melding of the natural temple.
Where his worship was simple and Stonehenge
A monument to all gracious in a God and Heaven.
Yes Stonehenge has become disassembled.
Hate me if you must though fate has
Exacted a toll far greater than any cost
Stonehenge has paid for loss of tribute.
And what Stonehenge has perchance
Failed in forgotten; it took Eurydice
To cause a backward glance from Orpheus,
And in that way only is the schema
Similar to the chain-y links of sin in ether.
So Stonehenge, I say, "Hate me if you must,"
But mourn the passing of your euphony more;
And remember how Stonehenge was when whole.
When all the folks there gathered round and
Beer and wine and heart full contemplation
Mattered still and was not a victim to vagrancies
Of youth before age and ere that woeful,
Woeful myopic-ity un-erected even
Such an ancient stony temple as thee.
   The componentry in the system
That was the Synagogue to Sangri-la
Has been whittled to one most solitary
Remaining tripped over monolith shorn
Of even the most primal purpose. All
That's left now is the hollow thrumming
Where in canyons can be distinguished
Only hollow echoes of the word "survival."
I for one shall mourn the passing,
Though long since our communion dampened,
And passions diverged from each other.
I remember! I remember when Stonehenge
Was beautiful; a symmetrical minion to
A mythical utopia where Pangaea had
Not yet been broken up. I recall then

When concentricity had a center and
The sparkle and the glitter of officious bars
Was not there to splinter a soul held consequential.
Now the circle has only a period for an ending,
Where I, for one, shall mourn the passing;
The bitter saddening of the losing--
And dismantling of that epic--Stonehenge.

Scribe

He's shocked; he's spent; he's lifted in
Uptight corners of animal tents; a circus.
No beauty in thy soul no matrimony at thy
Kirk of loving nuncios whose locution mentions
Love and passion and turbulent erections
Held in erotic check for the completion
Of all forms of frenetic coition: Sex!
All images adopt a brand-new obsolescence;
They=ve been painted before; See!
The words say the same thing; it=s just a
Dictionary; a manual held in verbal concupiscence.
Couldn't we climax one more time? Or are
The orgasms up in heaven and only humans
Left on the earth-world living; or can
We just divinely traverse the difference
Of female, male and mime only
To climax one more time?
The paints are dried and the strokes
Uneven and the tip tap on the keys
Sounds erratic and not symbolic of any sort of
Book, line or scene. God!
He places the weapon to his head and
Releases the projectile wishing to be
Far more than dead; does he die? Can he paint
Up in heaven or can he write when in hell?
Does the paper burn; does the missile turn
Or do all tinctures seep beneath the canvass
Of a landscape left un-imaged? And

Phonemes in Metaphors making scenes,
He sees—Fields where happy demons playing
Frost on midnight suns where the footprints
Of whores are remaining from angel pleasures.
--Scribe wakes up wishing he were dreaming,
And knowing Paradise is a walled-up symbol
Of Generals, Authority and men.

Coming Home

Coming home the funeral pyre is burning bright
Where that kayak slowly flows away down the canal
And he rests quietly in its solemn embrace;
No arrows shooting with flames attached to ignite the
Torch or shadow the surrounding banks with
Figures who dance with each lick of silent moonlight;
He leaves his home now where he built his fame
And all that made him was woven into each timber
And every trace carries the person; who he was
And his character and each sad line upon his face.
Back on the bank the house sits silently pondering
The absence of its maker and with each second what's
Left of him becomes more deeply deeply ingrained
In the nobility of the home's three-floor frame.
Every light is on as if expectation of his departure
Is written on the interior walls with the Chinese script
And lovely Goddess who protects the sanctity of home
And all who deign to enter within its pious walls.
He is gone now but all who know or knew him and
Celebrate within the home's interior space know that
With his silent passage down to the river's edge that
He, with all his torment, all his joys, and all his regrets
Is finally and with sighing breath—coming home.

Made in the USA
Columbia, SC
21 January 2024

25b15e1b-001b-45ec-9904-353a45195b5aR01